WATER-SKI WIPEOUT

Don't miss any of the cases in the Hardy Boys Clue Book series!

HARDY BOYS

→Clue Book← #3

WATER-SKI WIPEOUT

BY FRANKLIN W. DIXON ← → ILLUSTRATED BY MATT DAVID

ALADDIN
NEW YORK LONDON TORONTO SYDNEY NEW DELHI

This book is a work of fiction. Any references to historical events, real people,
or real places are used fictitiously. Other names, characters, places, and events are
products of the author's imagination, and any resemblance to actual events or
places or persons, living or dead, is entirely coincidental.

ALADDIN

An imprint of Simon & Schuster Children's Publishing Division
1230 Avenue of the Americas, New York, NY 10020
This Aladdin paperback edition August 2016
Text copyright © 2016 by Simon & Schuster, Inc.
Illustrations copyright © 2016 by Matt David
Also available in an Aladdin hardcover edition.
All rights reserved, including the right of reproduction in whole or in part in any form.
ALADDIN is a trademark of Simon & Schuster, Inc., and related logo is
a registered trademark of Simon & Schuster, Inc.
THE HARDY BOYS and colophons are registered trademarks of Simon & Schuster, Inc.
HARDY BOYS CLUE BOOK and colophons are trademarks of Simon & Schuster, Inc.
For information about special discounts for bulk purchases, please contact
Simon & Schuster Special Sales at 1-866-506-1949 or business@simonandschuster.com.
The Simon & Schuster Speakers Bureau can bring authors to your live event.
For more information or to book an event contact the Simon & Schuster Speakers Bureau
at 1-866-248-3049 or visit our website at www.simonspeakers.com.
Book designed by Karina Granda
The text of this book was set in Adobe Garamond Pro.
Manufactured in the United States of America 0419 OFF
4 6 8 10 9 7 5 3
Library of Congress Control Number 2016942233
ISBN 978-1-4814-5056-0 (hc)
ISBN 978-1-4814-5055-3 (pbk)
ISBN 978-1-4814-5057-7 (eBook)

CONTENTS

WATER-SKI WIPEOUT

Chapter 1

A CABIN IN THE WOODS

As the tour bus pulled up outside the lodge, Frank and Joe Hardy could see the lake in the distance. Bucks Mountain, the tallest peak near their hometown, Bayport, was right behind it.

"You think we could hike all the way to the top?" Frank asked, turning to his younger brother.

"It's probably too steep," eight-year-old Joe replied. "Besides, don't you want to spend all day out on the boat? That's why I brought the skis."

Nine-year-old Frank looked at the luggage rack above them. His brother's new water skis were tied together on the luggage rack with a bright blue strap. Last summer Joe had started water-skiing at camp. In just a few weeks, he'd gotten really good. He even tried to ski for a few seconds on just one ski—even though he usually ended up in the water! Joe was so excited about waterskiing, this year their parents had bought him his very own set of skis for Christmas. And he was ready to break them in at the third and fourth graders' school trip to Lake Poketoe. This would be the very first time he used them.

"You'll have to teach me," Frank said. "I doubt I'll be as good as you."

Ellie Freeman's head popped up over the seat in front of them. She was wearing her Bayport Bandits T-shirt. She was on their baseball team, and she liked wearing the uniform even when she didn't have to. "You promised to teach me too," she said, looking at Joe. "I want to learn how to do a flip!"

Joe laughed. "Like the professionals do? That's really hard. I don't think I'm going to be able to do that for a while!"

Ellie hopped out of her seat and grabbed her duffel bag from the rack above. "I guess I can try. . . . Are you guys going to the barbecue tonight?"

"You bet," Joe said. "Mr. Morton promised he'd make his famous smoked ribs." Mr. Morton, their good friend Chet's dad, was one of the parents who had come along on the school trip. Suzie Klein's mother had also come, but as far as Joe knew, she didn't make ribs as good as Mr. Morton's.

Joe reached for the water skis on the rack above, and they came down with a clatter as he tried to take them down.

"Ow! Watch it, Hardys."

Frank and Joe turned around to see Adam Ackerman in the seat behind them. Adam was in Frank's grade at school. He was sitting with his friend Paul. Adam was on the aisle, and he kept rubbing the side of his head.

"You hit me with those stupid skis!" Adam

complained. He stood up, yanking his bag down from the rack above. "You're going to pay for that, Hardy."

He pushed past them, nearly knocking Joe over. Paul followed close behind. He was a short boy with a large, round face. He always wore his brown baseball cap turned to the side. "Watch your back, Hardy," he grumbled.

"Just ignore them," Frank said. "It's not worth it."

But Joe's cheeks were hot. He felt like everyone on the bus was staring at him. "Let's go," he said, careful not to knock anyone else with the skis.

Adam was one of the biggest bullies at Bayport Elementary. He was taller than most of the kids and was always saying mean things or pushing people around. Frank and Joe tried to stay away from him, but even they had trouble with him sometimes.

The Hardys followed Ellie out of the bus, looking at the lake in front of them. A few kids had dropped their bags on the rocky beach. They crowded around Mrs. Jones, one of the parents who had come on the trip. She gave them directions as to which cabins were theirs. Frank and Joe found out they'd be staying in the lodge itself.

Just hearing the birds chirping put Joe in a better mood. The afternoon sun was out and the water looked cool and refreshing. A few yards away, a boat was zipping across the lake. A girl was in an inner tube behind it, screaming as it pulled her along.

"Frank and Joe Hardy! What a pleasant surprise!" Mrs. Rodriguez called out from the lodge. She'd been Joe's second-grade teacher, and she was one of the adults who'd come on the other bus. It was funny to see her in plaid shorts and a pink T-shirt. Joe hadn't ever seen her outside the classroom!

"This is the best!" Joe called out. "Glad we caught the last few hours of sunshine."

"It's good to have you here, just in case. . . . You never know what might happen!" Mrs. Rodriguez smiled. Just a few months ago Joe and Frank had helped her find a ring that she'd lost. She'd thought someone at school had stolen it, but the boys figured out that wasn't true. They eventually found it in one of her desk drawers.

It wasn't the first case they'd solved, though. Frank and Joe were known around Bayport for solving mysteries. Once it was a lost video game and another time it was a missing playbook. Their father, Fenton Hardy, was a private detective. He'd taught them everything they knew about investigating. He showed them how to interview suspects and search a crime scene for clues.

Joe dragged his water skis behind him. He was happy the path to the lodge wasn't that long—the skis were getting heavy! They followed the rest of their group into the lodge. There was a huge living room with couches. A few deer heads were on the wall above the fireplace.

"Whoa," Frank whispered. "That's kind of creepy."

"It's like a real log cabin," Joe said. He pointed to the ceiling, where you could see all the wood beams. It reminded him of the toys he and Frank played with when they were really little.

Frank looked out the back windows, toward the lake. There were a few small cabins there, hidden in the trees. He saw Adam and Paul go into one of them with their bags. A sign in the ground near the front said PINECONE CABIN.

Just then Chet Morton came down the hallway. "Did you guys pick your bunks yet?" he asked. "You should come check out our room! We left you a top and bottom bunk!"

They followed him down the hall, to a room with two sets of bunk beds. Mr. Morton was sitting on one. He pulled a jar of red stuff from his bag. "My secret rib sauce!" He smiled. "I'll need this for tonight."

Frank and Joe laughed. "I call dibs on the top bunk!" Joe declared. He looked around, realizing there wasn't a good place to leave his skis. "Where should I put these?" he asked. "They take up the whole room."

"There's a shed out back," Chet said. "Here, I'll show you."

As Chet ran out the door, his dad called after him. "You can go explore, but make sure you're back in an hour. Dinner will be served!"

Chet showed Frank and Joe the storage shed behind the lodge. There were a dozen other cabins around it. Joe put his skis inside, next to a pile of life vests. Then the boys followed Chet down to the dock.

"Wow, there are kayaks!" Frank said.

"And we can use that tomorrow morning," Chet added, pointing to a white speedboat tied to the dock. "Joe, remember, you promised me you'd teach me to water ski!"

"He promised you . . . and me . . . and Ellie . . . and half the school," Frank laughed. "It's going to be a long day."

Joe smiled as they walked back to the lodge. A crowd had gathered on the deck. Mr. Morton, Mrs. Rodriguez, and some of the other adults were cooking dinner. Some kids were sitting at the round tables, drinking lemonade. Ellie and a few of her friends were tossing a softball back and forth on the grass below.

As the sun set, Joe could almost picture what it would be like tomorrow. All his friends would be out on the boat. He'd teach them how to do different tricks on his water skis. Maybe they'd even go tubing afterward.

"Who's ready to eat?" Mr. Morton called out. A bunch of kids cheered.

Joe, Frank, and Chet all cheered along with them. One thing was certain: this was going to be the best school trip yet.

Chapter 2.

CHOOSE YOUR OWN ADVENTURE

"Today we'll have three groups heading out," Mr. Morton told everyone the next morning when they'd gathered at picnic tables outside the lodge for breakfast. "Mrs. Rodriguez will be taking a group to the other side of the lake, to hike Bucks Mountain. You'll learn about all the wildlife in this region and collect samples of leaves from trees native to this forest. All of you have to go at some point, either today or tomorrow."

"Awesome!" Billy Krueger called out. He was in the same class as Frank and always seemed to have a smile on his face. "I want to see a bear! I'm in!"

Mr. Morton laughed. "Wait one minute—I'm not done yet. Mrs. Pinkelton will be doing nature crafts in the lodge this morning, and I'll take a group out on the boat. She'll be doing fish, leaf, and flower prints. I'll take you tubing and skiing, yes, but then I'll take you guys past Seaway Island, home to Native American artifacts. After lunch, we'll switch groups so everyone gets to do two different activities today."

Ellie Freeman raised her hand and called out, "Is Joe Hardy going out on the boat this morning?"

Mr. Morton pointed to Joe, who was sitting at one of the tables, eating breakfast with Frank and Chet. "You'll have to ask him." Then he went inside the lodge.

Joe had a forkful of eggs in his mouth. Before he could even look up, Ellie and four of her friends were around the table. Two of the girls were on the Bayport club soccer team. Joe recognized their blue-and-white T-shirts. "Can we borrow your water skis too?" a girl with blond pigtails asked.

Joe swallowed his bite. "Sure."

"Our friends Jack and Connor want to come out on the boat, but only if they can water-ski too. Is that okay?" a girl with freckles asked.

Frank smiled. "Everyone can come. Joe will give waterskiing lessons to everyone!"

Ellie and her friends seemed happy at that answer. Then they turned to go. They stopped at the buffet table and picked up some fruit salad and English muffins on their way. When Frank saw them sit down a few tables away, he leaned over to Chet and Joe. "Looks like everyone's heard about your water-skiing skills," he laughed.

"You're the most popular kid here this weekend!" Chet said. "You're going to be on the boat all day today and tomorrow."

"That's okay with me," Joe said. The truth was, he couldn't have been more excited. He hadn't been on a boat since camp last year. All winter he and Frank had talked about this trip, how it would be so cool to be at Lake Poketoe all weekend, with a bunch of their friends. Even though they had to do some school stuff, they were super psyched to go waterskiing and tubing on the lake. And then they could make s'mores around the campfire at night. It wasn't even ten o'clock yet, but already the day was great. It was almost better than he'd imagined.

A few kids at the table next to them stood and

dropped their paper plates in the garbage. Another group had gone down to the lawn below and were throwing a Frisbee. Some others played tag through the trees. Within a few minutes, Mr. Morton came outside. "Has everyone decided? Who will be going to Bucks Mountain to hike?"

A dozen kids raised their hands, then left with Mrs. Rodriguez. She was saying something about bears and rattlesnakes as they walked off. Another big group went inside to do arts and crafts, and soon Mr. Morton's group headed toward the water.

"This is going to be incredible," Ellie said. "I'm so excited!"

"I've never been on a boat before," her redheaded friend, Nina, said.

"Where did you get your water skis?" a boy named Charlie asked.

"Our parents got them for him," Frank said, answering for Joe.

"Now let's get those skis and some life vests," Mr. Morton added.

Frank and Joe led the way to the shed, moving

deeper into the forest. There were log cabins every few yards. Some were just one room, while a few others were two stories high. When they got to the shed, Mr. Morton opened it, then pulled some of the life vests out.

He handed one to each kid, but when he got to Joe, he said, "You put your water skis in the shed last night, right? Why don't you go in and get them?"

Joe peered into the shed. There were only a few life vests there, along with an inner tube and neon-green foam noodles. He pushed inside, moving things around. He knelt down to see if his skis had fallen, but they weren't on the floor. They weren't anywhere.

"What is it?" Frank asked. He stood in the doorway, his brow furrowed.

"My skis," Joe yelled. "They're gone!"

Chapter 3

GONE WITHOUT A TRACE

"They have to be here somewhere," Mr. Morton said, scratching his head. He knelt down, looking at the same exact spot Joe had looked at just seconds before. He shook his head. Then he stood on his tiptoes and checked the top shelf. "Hmmm," he muttered.

Behind him, the rest of the group had started whispering to one another. Charlie leaned over to the girl next to him and said something about the skis being stolen. The girl nodded.

"But who would steal them?" Chet asked, overhearing their conversation. He walked around the back of the shed, checking to see if the skis had been put somewhere else. Joe followed behind, but there was just an old shovel and two rakes.

"Now, now," Mr. Morton said. "Let's not jump to conclusions. Are you sure this is where you put them?"

Joe glanced sideways at his brother. Frank nodded. The sun had been going down when they dropped the skis off, but they were certain it was here. There weren't any other sheds in this part of the woods. There were only lots of cabins and lots of trees.

"I'm very sure," Joe insisted. "Frank and Chet walked me here last night, and I put them inside. I closed the door behind me. They were right there. They were right next to the life vests." He pointed to the spot where he'd left them.

"What are we going to do?" Ellie asked.

"I guess we can't go out on the boat now," Charlie said. A few of the other kids groaned.

"We can still go out . . . you'll just have to go

tubing," Mr. Morton said. "Maybe you'll find the skis tonight and you can water-ski tomorrow."

Joe looked at his brother and frowned. The school trip was only three days long, and now they were losing one whole day. "I can't believe this is happening," Joe said sadly. "I've been excited about this trip for months."

"We'll find them," Frank said. He hadn't seen Joe this upset since the Bandits lost their championship game. He patted his brother on the shoulder, trying to make him feel better.

"Someone must've stolen them," Joe declared. "They didn't just disappear."

Chet looked around at the woods. "But who would do that?" he asked.

"I think I know who," Joe said, his voice sad.

Frank looked at the crowd of kids standing around them. Some had towels slung over their shoulders. A few others had already put on their life vests. "Why don't you take the rest of the group out?" Frank said to Mr. Morton. "Hopefully, by the time you get back, we will have found the skis."

Mr. Morton looked back at the lodge, as if he were considering it. "Okay. . . . If you need anything, Mrs. Pinkelton is right there in the lodge. She'll be there if you need any help."

Ellie frowned as she walked down toward the dock. "Good luck," she said. "We'll miss you out there."

A few of her friends turned to wave too. Some boys moaned about how weird it was that the skis were missing, and a few others wondered who had taken them. Charlie kept saying he couldn't believe it.

"You don't have to stay behind," Frank said, turning to Chet.

Chet smiled. "It's the least I can do. I can't believe this either."

Frank glanced at his brother, who had slumped down against the side of the shed. He looked miserable. "We'll find them," he promised.

"Right," Joe mumbled. "But how?"

Chapter 4

THE FIVE WS

Frank walked over to his brother and held out his hand. "Come on," he said. "Let's get to work."

Joe grabbed a notebook and pencil from the back pocket of his shorts. He always kept them on him just in case. Sometimes he used them to write down things he remembered about other cases, or funny things he'd seen. Other times he needed them for an investigation like this one.

"The five Ws," Joe said. "Who, What, When, Where, and Why."

He scribbled the words down the side of the page. Their dad had taught them that this list was a good way to start investigating a case. Sometimes you knew what was taken, but not where it was taken from. Other times you knew when, but not why.

"Who . . . ," Joe said, annoyed. He wrote down *Adam Ackerman* and underlined it. "That's easy. Case solved."

He turned the notebook around and showed Frank and Chet his answer. Frank just sighed. "Come on," he said. "You know it's never that simple."

Chet furrowed his brow. "Why are you so sure it was Adam?"

Joe crossed his arms over his chest. "When we were getting off the bus, I knocked him in the head with the skis. He said, 'You're going to pay for that, Hardy.' What better way to punish me than to take the skis?"

"You can write down 'maybe' next to his name," Frank said. "But this doesn't seem like something Adam would do. It would be too obvious. He'd know we'd all suspect him."

Joe added *(Maybe)* after Adam's name. He had a feeling Frank was right. But still, he couldn't forget Adam's face as the bully pushed past him and off the bus. He'd seemed so mad. Was he mad enough to take the water skis? Would he really do that?

Frank went into the shed, waving for Chet and

Joe to follow. "Let's stick to the facts for now. Why don't you remind us exactly when you put them in the shed?"

Joe walked over to the place where the life vests were. "I leaned them against these shelves right here. I came in right after we arrived."

"They were taken sometime between six o'clock last night and ten o'clock this morning," Chet added. He pointed to the word *When?* on Joe's paper. Joe wrote down the times.

Joe wrote down notes as he talked. Next to *Where?* he wrote: *Storage shed behind the lodge.* Beneath that, he wrote: *They were leaning against the shelves, on the right side of the shed.*

Frank paced back and forth. "Now let's think of *why*," he said.

"They were expensive," Joe said. "Maybe someone wanted to sell them."

"Or it could be because Adam was mad," Chet added. "Just like you said."

Frank scratched his head. "Maybe someone is playing a joke on you. But that doesn't seem likely."

Joe wrote down all the reasons why someone might've wanted to take the skis. His dad liked to call this a "motive." A motive was a reason why someone would commit a crime.

"'*What*,'" Joe said. "That's easy. My water skis." He wrote down a short description of the skis, including that they were tied with a blue strap. When he was done, he looked down the list. They didn't have much information about this case. If Adam Ackerman hadn't taken the skis, who had?

Chet knelt down by the shed door. He was looking at a yellow towel crumpled on the floor. "Could this be a clue?" he asked.

Frank picked up the towel, noticing it had the letters SLSG written across the top in big black print. "Maybe," he said. "It's hard to tell how long it's been here. I have no idea what 'SLSG' means."

Joe flipped to a clean page in his notebook and wrote down *Yellow towel—SLSG*. "We should probably write down everything in here, just in case," he said. He counted an oar, a life tube, three extra life vests, and the foam noodles. Then he

wrote everything down in a list. When he was done, Frank and Chet came to his side, reading over the notes with him. Chet crossed his arms over his chest. "Where should we start?" he asked.

Frank turned and looked out the shed door toward the lodge. The closest cabin to the shed was only a few yards away. The sign in front read PINECONE CABIN. He recognized it instantly.

He stared out over the lake toward Bucks Mountain. Mrs. Rodriguez had left less than half an hour ago. He'd seen Adam and Paul go with her. Maybe it was unlikely that Adam had taken the skis, but that was the same cabin he'd seen Paul and Adam go into last night. Besides, it was their only real lead.

Frank pointed at the path that led into the woods. "Let's go that way," he said. "If we're fast, we can probably catch Mrs. Rodriguez's group before they get to the other side of the lake."

Chet followed behind as Joe and Frank took off down the trail. "I'm confused. . . . Why do we want to catch them?" he called out.

"Adam's in that group," Frank said.

"I thought you didn't think it was him," Chet said.

Frank ran faster, waving for Chet to hurry up. "It probably wasn't. But if he's the only one on our suspect list, we might as well be sure. Once we know he didn't steal them—"

"Then we can find out who did," Joe finished. He smiled as he ran past his brother, moving deeper into the woods.

Chapter 5

THEY'RE HIDING SOMETHING

They'd been running for a while when they spotted the group up ahead. The kids, led by Mrs. Rodriguez, turned and took the trail down toward the beach. Frank and Joe could see Adam and Paul in the back, walking along behind the others. The two boys were each carrying a stick, which they used to swat away the tree branches.

"Hey!" Frank called out. "Wait for us!"

The whole group turned around, studying the

boys. Mrs. Rodriguez smiled. "Where did you boys come from? I thought you were going out on the boat today," she said. "Is everything all right?"

When Frank, Joe, and Chet finally caught up, they were out of breath. "We're fine. Mr. Morton said we could hang around the lodge as long as Mrs. Pinkelton knew where we were. We aren't going on the hike," Joe said. "We were just hoping to talk to Adam for a second."

Mrs. Rodriguez nodded. "I guess that's fine. Be careful, though—you missed my warning. There are rattlesnakes in these woods. There are also brown bears. I don't think we'll run into one, but make sure you make a lot of noise. The last thing we want is to sneak up on one."

The group started back down the trail. Frank noticed that a few kids in the front had sticks too. They banged them together as they walked, making noise.

"What do you want?" Adam asked. He didn't look at them as he talked.

"We just wanted to ask you a few questions," Chet said.

Adam and Paul laughed. "Is this for another one of your little mysteries?"

Joe took a deep breath to calm himself down. He didn't like how Adam said those words. He was always making fun of the Hardys, even when he didn't mean to. "We know you took my skis," Joe said. "Where did you put them?"

Adam scrunched his nose. "Your skis? What are you talking about?"

Frank glanced sideways at his brother. Joe was letting Adam get to him. Just because Adam and Paul were staying in the cabin near the shed, that didn't mean Adam definitely had taken the skis. It didn't mean anything that he had been rude to Joe, either.

Frank tried a different strategy. "We noticed your cabin was near the storage shed. Did you see anything strange last night?"

Paul laughed. "What are you guys even talking about?"

"Joe's water skis are missing," Chet explained. "And yesterday, on the bus, you got really mad at him. You told him you'd get back at him for hitting you with his skis."

Adam rubbed his head like he didn't remember. "Oh . . . that."

Joe was so mad, his cheeks were red. "Did you take them? Don't lie to us."

Adam shook his head. "I didn't, I swear."

Paul stopped walking. He turned, looking at Frank and Joe for the first time. "We definitely didn't take them. When Adam said that, we were going to play a prank on you or something. Pull your chair out when you tried to sit down. Something like that."

Frank stepped toward his brother. He was starting to feel really annoyed. Why did Adam always have to be so mean?

"Well, if you didn't take them," Chet said, "who did?"

"Look, we didn't see anything weird," Adam said. "I don't know anything about this."

Paul stood still. He looked at Frank and Joe like he wanted to say something, but he didn't. Then

Adam nudged him. "Come on, let's go," he said, pulling Paul along behind him.

Adam and Paul turned, following the rest of the group up the path.

"That was weird," Chet said. "Didn't it seem like Paul wanted to tell us something?"

"Definitely," Joe said. "He knows something."

Frank sighed. "It's like he was afraid to say it in front of Adam."

The boys walked back toward the shed. Joe looked down at his notebook, going through all the clues they had. It was possible the person who took the skis had something to do with the yellow towel, but they couldn't be sure. Now the best thing to do would be to go back to the shed and see if there was anything they'd missed.

They hadn't gotten very far when they heard footsteps behind them. They turned and saw Paul running toward them. He looked nervous.

"Hey, guys," he said. "I don't have much time, but I wanted to tell you I did see something. Last night I got out of bed and saw a boy walking down toward the lake with your skis. I just thought it was you."

"What did he look like?" Joe asked.

"He had on a black hooded sweatshirt," Paul said. "He had your skis—I saw them."

"Are you sure?" Frank asked.

"Positive," Paul said.

Frank looked at Joe and smiled. Maybe it hadn't been such a bad idea to start with Adam. It wasn't even eleven o'clock and they already had a break in the case. Paul Alcotti was now their very first witness.

Chapter 6

THE SUSPECT

Joe flipped his notebook to a clean page. He wrote the word *Who?* again, and *Possible suspect* beside it. "Tell us everything you remember," Joe said.

Paul rubbed his hands together like he was nervous. He glanced over his shoulder. The group was behind him, moving along a trail by the beach. "Umm . . ."

Frank saw how worried Paul seemed. Adam was at the back of the group. He hadn't noticed Paul was gone yet.

"If you don't want anyone to know you told us, that's okay," Frank said. "We can keep it a secret."

Paul nodded. "Yeah, I just . . . I don't want Adam know I'm helping you guys. He'd be mad, you know?"

"It's okay," Frank said. Their dad had taught them that sometimes witnesses didn't like anyone to know they'd helped with a case. Maybe it was because they knew the suspect, or maybe they were scared the suspect might get mad at them. Mr. Hardy told Frank and Joe it was okay to keep what they said a secret.

"So we were hanging out in our cabin. And I got out of bed and went to the bathroom," Paul began. "I was looking out the window and I saw this kid. He was walking out of the shed with the skis. I didn't think it was weird at first, but then when you said someone had stolen them . . ."

Chet put his hands on his hips. "That's crazy!" he said. "Who was this guy? What did he look like?"

Paul rubbed his head. "Like I said, he had a black

hooded sweatshirt on. He was wearing jeans. I think he had light hair . . . like blond. And he looked short."

Joe wrote down everything Paul said. "Do you remember what time it was?"

Paul bit his lip. "Maybe nine thirty. It was just after lights-out—that I remember."

"Where was he heading?" Frank asked. "Did you see where he went?"

"He was going toward the dock . . . ," Paul said. He opened his mouth to say something else, but then someone called out from the forest behind him.

"Paul! Where'd you go? Are you there?"

Paul's eyes went wide when he heard Adam's voice. "I gotta go!" he said, turning to run back. "I'll see you guys later!"

The boys watched as Paul ran back toward the group. "I'm coming!" he called out to Adam. "I just got lost!"

Within a few seconds he was gone. Frank turned to Joe. "We officially have a suspect," he said. "We're getting closer, I can feel it. Hopefully, we'll find your skis and be out on the lake this afternoon."

Joe smiled. "I hope," he said. "Let's go back to the shed and see if we missed anything. We have to find that boy."

Ten minutes later Frank, Chet, and Joe were back at the shed. They walked around it, looking for any clues they might have missed.

"Nine thirty," Chet mumbled. "The thief was out late. He must've waited until everyone was in their bunks for the night."

Joe stopped by a corner of the shed. He barely heard what Chet had just said. He was too busy studying some tracks that led down to the beach. "Look at these," he said. "We must've missed them before."

Frank came around the side of the shed. There was one long line that started a few yards away. "The edge of the skis must've dug into the dirt," he said, following it.

They walked beside the tracks, noticing that they went toward the dock. Halfway to the dock the lines changed. There were two lines, not one.

They were about a foot away from each other.

"He started by carrying them," Frank said. "That's why there were no lines. Then he dragged them together. Then he took them apart and dragged one in each hand."

Chet knelt down. He picked something blue out of a pile of dead leaves. "Is this something?" he asked.

Joe perked up when he saw the blue strap. "That's what held the skis together!" he said. "We're definitely close."

Chet passed the blue strap to Joe, who put it in his pocket. They followed the tracks all the way down to the beach, where they ended right at the dock. There were a few girls swimming in the water. Another group was sitting in a speedboat, reading. One of the girls, in a pink sundress, was weaving a friendship bracelet with colorful string. Behind them, an older woman in a giant white hat thumbed through a magazine.

Frank stopped before the girls noticed them. "This might be it," he said. "Maybe the thief used this boat to water-ski. That would make sense, right?"

Before Joe could answer, the girl in the pink sundress turned around. She was a little older than the boys, maybe ten. "What's up?" she said. She put down the bracelet she was making.

Frank stepped forward. "We were wondering if you've seen a boy in a black hooded sweatshirt and jeans. He was definitely wearing those last night, and maybe even today, too. He has light hair and is pretty short."

The girl just shrugged. One of her friends was lying out on a yellow towel. Another one was drinking a soda.

"I didn't see anyone like that," the girl in the sundress said. "But we just got here last night."

"What time?" Frank asked.

"Like eight o'clock," another girl said. "This is our first day here, and it's been quiet all morning."

"Is this the only boat at this dock?" Chet asked.

"There's been a few boats going in and out," the girl said.

Joe wrote down what she said in his notebook. He was glad Chet had asked her that question. Just because the thief took the skis down to this dock didn't mean he got on this boat. He could have used any of the boats that left from here.

"But you didn't see a boy by that description? He might have had water skis with him," Frank said.

Another girl turned around. She was wearing

a yellow sweatshirt with the words SAINT LILAC SCHOOL FOR GIRLS across the front. "There were some boys," she said. "But no one who looked like that. It was dark by the time we got here last night, though."

"Did you see anything strange?" Chet asked.

The girls shook their heads.

Joe let out a deep breath. He knew the boy had probably changed out of whatever he was wearing last night. They'd have better luck if they questioned people at the lodge. But who would remember seeing a boy in a black sweatshirt? Half the third- and fourth-grade boys from Bayport Elementary were wearing dark sweatshirts last night.

"Thanks," Joe said. "Let us know if you remember anything. We're staying back there." He pointed to the lodge.

The boys turned and walked back to the lodge, more confused than ever.

"The lines lead right to the dock," Chet pointed out. "He must've brought the skis there."

"But he could be anyone," Frank said. "We don't

have a good enough description of him. Paul saw him from so far away."

Joe scanned the woods. "We have to have missed something," he said.

Frank looked around. "Yeah," he agreed. "But what?"

Chapter 7

MISTAKEN IDENTITY

Frank knew something wasn't right. Sometimes he got a nagging feeling that they'd asked the wrong questions, or that they were looking in the wrong places. There was something about this case that they had missed.

The boys walked through the woods in silence. Frank glanced up the hill, noticing the cabin Adam and Paul had stayed in. It said PINECONE CABIN above the door. Paul hadn't given them a great description. But where had he been standing? Had he seen everything clearly?

"I just want to check something," Frank said, walking toward it.

When he got there, the front door was open. He crept inside, Chet and Joe following close behind him. There were four bedrooms spread out off the main living area.

"Paul said he was staying in that room in the corner," Joe whispered. He had his notebook out and was looking at his notes.

"Which means he probably used the bathroom that's right near it," Chet said.

The three boys climbed the stairs. The cabin was much dirtier than the main lodge. There were some cobwebs near the ceilings, and mud tracked across the floor. When they got upstairs, they went into the tiny bathroom. There was only one window, and it was covered with dirt.

"He saw the boy from here? At night?" Chet asked. "It's the middle of the day and I can barely see out of this window!"

Frank leaned forward, putting his nose close to the glass. "Exactly," he said.

"Whatever he saw," Joe added, "it can't be trusted."

Frank stood up straight. "He probably did see someone in a black hooded sweatshirt," he said. "He'd be able to tell his height."

Joe's eyes widened. He cupped his hand over his mouth, like he'd just remembered something. "I know what we missed!" he said. "It all makes sense now."

"What?" Chet asked.

"SLSG!" Joe said. "The yellow towel!"

Frank and Chet almost laughed. "Huh?" Frank said. "What about it?"

Joe was so excited, he started talking twice as fast as normal. "When we went down to the dock and saw those girls. One of them was sitting on a yellow towel. And the other girl was wearing a sweatshirt that said Saint Lilac School for Girls."

"Wait . . . SLSG," Frank repeated. He couldn't help but smile. Joe had figured it out. They'd missed one important clue. "The towel from the shed belonged to a girl."

Chet looked confused. "I don't understand," he said.

"SLSG stands for Saint Lilac School for Girls," Joe said. "The girls only got to the lake last night. So whoever left the towel in the shed was there between eight o'clock last night and ten o'clock this morning. Right when the water skis were stolen."

"This whole time we've been looking for a boy in a hooded sweatshirt," Frank said. "And Paul didn't even see the person clearly."

Chet laughed. "I can't believe it!" he said. "We've been looking for a boy . . . when we should've been looking for a girl!"

"Exactly," Joe said. "We need to go back to the dock and talk to those girls again, before it's too late."

Joe ran down the stairs, more excited than ever. They were getting

so close to solving the case. Maybe they didn't know who their suspect was, but at least they knew what school she went to, and who she was hanging out with. With a little luck, they'd be out water-skiing by the end of the day.

Chapter

8

THE NEW GIRL

By the time the boys got back to the dock, the girls were packing up their things. One girl stuffed her towel and book in a straw bag. Another pulled some neon foam noodles out of the water.

"Hey, Annie, can you pass me my magazines?" one of the girls asked.

As a girl in a sundress turned to grab the magazines, she saw the boys.

"It's you guys again," Annie said. "Did you find that kid?"

"Well . . . ," Frank started. "We may have made a mistake. We don't think it's a boy we're looking for. We think it's a girl. And we think she goes to your school."

Annie frowned. "What do you mean?"

A few of her friends had climbed out of the water and onto the dock. They were drying off while they listened to what the boys were saying. One girl raised her eyebrows.

"We might have gotten things confused," Joe said. He stopped there, not wanting to tell them too much. There was a chance their suspect was one of the girls they were talking to.

He looked around, studying the girls' faces. They all seemed nice enough. Then he noticed their hair. There were eight of them standing around the dock, but only two of them had light hair. Both of those two girls were taller than most girls their age.

Earlier, Paul had described the suspect as being

short with light hair, and the boys had agreed that that was probably right, even if it was dark and the window was dirty. He still would've been able to see how tall she was. Was it okay to tell the girls more? Could they risk it?

Before Joe could decide, Chet blurted out another question. "Did you see a girl with water skis?"

Frank glanced sideways at his brother. This was sometimes the problem with having friends help during a case. They didn't always know which parts of the story they shouldn't share with people.

"We think the girl in the black hooded sweatshirt may have taken a pair of water skis," Joe explained. "Does any of this sound familiar?"

Annie started laughing. "I knew she was up to something!" she said.

A girl with a black braid added, "I can't believe this is happening."

"What?" Frank asked. "Who are you talking about?"

Annie sat down on the dock. "And she was being so weird last night," she remembered. Then she turned to the boys. "I think you're looking for the new girl . . . Trixie? No, wait, it's Trina."

Joe pulled out his notebook and wrote down the names with a question mark next to each one. "Why do you think it's her? She's short with light hair?"

"And she was acting so weird last night!" the girl with the braid said. "She's always acting weird, but this was different."

Frank scratched his head. "What do you mean? Did you see her with the water skis?"

"No . . . but that doesn't matter. Everyone else was playing board games in our cabin," Annie said. "And out of nowhere, Trina and this other girl said they had to leave. But they wouldn't tell us where they were going."

Joe wrote down all the details, nodding. It did sound like strange behavior. "So the girls went together? Do you remember her friend's name?"

The girl with the black braid answered, "Well . . . I doubt they're friends. The other girl is named Sara Carter."

A few of the other girls giggled. Frank glanced sideways at his brother. It was starting to seem like the rest of the girls didn't like Trina very much. He felt bad that they were laughing at her behind her back.

"It's just . . . ," Annie said. "Trina doesn't have many friends. She's only been at school a week."

"Do any of you know her?" Frank asked.

The girls shook their heads. "No . . . not really," Annie said.

"Do you know where she is right now?" Chet said.

A girl with pigtails told the boys, "We haven't seen her since this morning."

"I saw her!" a redheaded girl said. "Right after breakfast. She was by our cabin."

Joe wrote down *Last seen near SLSG cabin*. Then he asked, "Where is your cabin? Does it have a name?"

"We're in the Oaks," Annie said. She slung her polka-dotted towel around her shoulder as she spoke. Then she pointed into the woods. "It's the red cabin. It's a five-minute walk that way."

Frank looked at Chet and his brother, then back out over the lake. The sun was high in the sky, and it was close to noon. But Mr. Morton hadn't come back yet with the boat and the rest of the group. "We should go to that cabin now," Frank said. "We still have a lot to figure out."

The boys thanked the Saint Lilac girls and

headed off into the woods. "There are still so many questions about the motive," Joe said, looking down at his notebook. "Even if it is Trina, we still don't know why she did it. What would she want with my water skis?"

"Be careful," Frank said. "We don't actually know if it's Trina, remember? The girls didn't see her with the skis."

Joe flipped through his notes again. Reading through them, he realized Frank was right. They'd asked if the girls had seen Trina with the skis, but they hadn't. The girls were only certain of a few things: that she was acting weird, that she didn't have a lot of friends, and that they didn't know her.

"But if they don't know her, why do they think she was acting weird? How would they know that?" Joe asked.

Frank nodded. "And if they're not friends with her or they don't like her very much, they might think she did something she didn't do."

Chet turned back to look at the lake as they walked. "We'll get to the bottom of this," he said.

"By tomorrow we'll be out on the lake, water-skiing with our friends."

"I hope," Frank said.

But as Joe looked back at the sun in the sky, he wasn't so sure. How could they know if it was Trina who'd taken the skis? And even if she had taken them, where were they now? Would Joe ever see them again?

Chapter 9

TWISTS AND TURNS

When they got to the red cabin, there were two girls sitting on the deck. One had a giant bowl of grapes, and another was eating the last of her cheeseburger. The one with the grapes had reddish-brown hair, and the other had dark eyes and black hair. Neither of them fit the description of Trina.

"We were hoping you could help us," Frank said, climbing up the stairs. "Do you know a girl named Trina? She's new to your school?"

The girl with black hair narrowed her eyes. "The only girl who's new is named Tamara. Is that who you mean?"

Before Frank could respond, the girl got up and went to the door. "Tamara!" she called inside. "Someone is looking for you!"

Within minutes, a short girl with a blond bob came to the door. She looked confused. "Who's looking for me?" she asked. "What's wrong?"

Joe stepped forward. "I'm Joe and this is my brother, Frank. We're from Bayport Elementary," he explained. "We're staying at another cabin on the lake, on the other side of the woods. We were hoping to ask you some questions."

Tamara shrugged. "Sure. I guess that's fine. What's wrong?"

The two other girls went back to their snacks. They started talking about joining the Saint Lilac basketball team. Tamara came outside and sat down on the deck stairs. She put her chin in her hands.

"We heard you're new in school," Frank said. "Is that true?"

Tamara looked puzzled. "Yeah . . . why?"

"We're trying to solve a mystery," Chet said. "And we've been going around, asking if anyone saw anything strange. Someone said you might know something."

"Who?" Tamara asked.

Chet pointed back to the dock. "Just some of the girls down by the dock. They told us your name was Trina."

"They don't even know my name," Tamara said sadly. "What did they say about me?"

"What were you doing last night after eight o'clock?" Joe asked. "Were you here, in your cabin?"

Tamara scratched her head. "Yeah . . . I think so. We got in around eight thirty, and then everyone had dinner together. Then some people were hanging out. I took a walk, but that's about it."

Joe looked at his brother. It didn't seem like Tamara was trying to hide anything. If she had stolen the skis, it would be odd for her to admit that she'd left the cabin last night. "Did you see anything strange?" he asked.

"No," she said. "My friend and I were just walking and talking. I just didn't want to be around everybody last night. I felt like people were laughing at me."

She looked sad when she said it. Joe was going to ask another question, but then he noticed a girl looking out the window of the cabin. She had light blond pigtails. "Is that your friend?" he said.

Tamara turned around and waved at the girl. "Yeah, that's Sara. She's been really nice to me since I've gotten here. She's the one I went on the walk with."

Frank turned back to Tamara. "We're looking for a pair of water skis," he said. "Do you know anything about that?"

Tamara shook her head. "No. Who lost them?"

"We think they were stolen," Joe said. "They were mine."

"I'm sorry about that," Tamara said. "That's such a bummer. I used to water-ski in my old town. I used to live right on a lake. I really loved it."

"Yeah, it's the best," Joe added. He kept looking

at Sara. She was still watching them from the window. She looked curious as she watched them talk.

Then Sara opened the window. "Tamara!" she called. "We need your help with something! Can you come here?"

Tamara turned back toward the cabin. "I guess I have to go," she said. She smiled at the boys. "Good luck with everything. I hope you find your skis."

With that, she ran up the stairs. The boys walked a few feet away, where the other girls couldn't hear them. "It definitely felt like Tamara was telling the truth," Chet said. "She didn't seem like she has anything to hide."

"I agree," Frank said. "I'm more interested in Sara. . . ."

Joe turned back toward the house. Sara was still at the window. She walked away when she noticed him. "Did you see she has blond hair?" Joe asked.

"She and Tamara look very similar," Frank said. "And she doesn't look very tall either. Which means . . ."

"She could've been the one that Paul saw!" Chet said.

Frank walked ahead of them, into the woods. He waved for them to come hide behind a big tree. "I have an idea," he said.

Chet and Joe crouched down beside him. Chet peered back toward the cabin. The two girls who were sitting on the deck had gone inside.

"If our suspicions are right," Frank said, "Sara is worried about us. And when a suspect is worried they might get caught, they sometimes get sloppy."

"Like the time we caught Lester Pinks," Joe said. Lester had been taking tickets from Fun World, an arcade in Bayport. He'd gotten so nervous after Frank and Joe questioned him that he started covering his tracks. Frank and Joe had been watching him and saw where he'd hidden all the prizes.

"Exactly," Frank said. "We should wait here. I have a hunch that if Sara was the one who took the skis, she'll make her next move soon."

The boys sat down behind the big tree, leaning their backs against it. Time was going by. They only had an hour before they had to be back for lunch. After a while Joe got tired. His eyes started to close, and he fell fast asleep.

"Joe! Wake up! Look!" Frank whispered.

Joe rubbed his eyes. He wasn't sure how long he'd been napping. He peered out from behind the tree. Sara was crawling out from underneath the deck of the cabin. "What happened?" he asked.

"She just went under there. . . . She must be hiding something," Chet said.

Sara looked around the woods before she turned toward the lake. Then she took off down a trail.

"Come on," Frank said. He rushed toward the cabin. When he got to the deck he crawled underneath it, feeling around beneath the dead leaves.

"What's there?" Joe asked. "Did you find anything?"

Frank moved farther under the deck. The light outside the cabin came through the slats in the deck. He could see one ski, but not the other. He pushed the dead leaves and dirt around, but he still couldn't find the other one. It wasn't there.

He crawled back out and handed the ski to Joe. "My ski!" Joe cried.

"Where's the other one?" Chet asked.

"It's not under there," Frank said. He pointed toward the path where Sara had gone. "We have to find her. She knows what happened, and she probably knows where that other ski is."

Joe hid his one ski under the deck again, and the three boys took off through the woods. They ran as fast as they could. By the time they saw Sara up ahead, they were almost out of breath. "Wait! Stop! We need to talk to you!"

Sara turned back, but when she saw who was following her, she started running. She darted down the path toward the beach.

"She's getting away!" Chet cried. "We have to stop her!"

The boys ran even faster. They jumped over fallen trees and rocks. They followed her left through the woods, then right.

Finally she turned toward the beach. The dock was on one side of her, and they were on the other. Sara finally stopped and sat down in the sand.

"We just want to ask you something," Joe panted, out of breath from running. "We think you might be able to help us find the skis."

Sara put her hands up and looked sad. "I'm sorry," she said. Her eyes were brimming with tears. "I can explain, I swear. . . ."

THE HARDY BOYS—and
YOU!

CAN YOU SOLVE THE MYSTERY OF THE MISSING SKIS?

Grab a piece of paper and write your answers down.
Or just turn the page to find out!

1. Frank and Joe came up with a list of suspects.
    Can you think of more? List your suspects.

2. Which clues helped you to solve this mystery?
    Write them down.

Chapter
10

A FRIEND IN NEED

Sara put her face in her hands. For a moment, Frank and Joe almost felt bad for her.

"I'm sorry," she said again. "I really am. I didn't mean to."

"What happened?" Joe asked.

The boys stood there, looking at Sara. Out on the lake, they could see the light of a boat coming toward them. Joe wondered if it was Mr. Morton and the rest of the group, but they were too far away to see.

Sara let out a deep breath. "I was just trying to help Tamara. She's new, and she's been having a really hard time. Some of the girls are mean to her. Last night she was upset, and we went for a walk. She was talking about her old town, and things she liked to do there—"

"And she mentioned waterskiing," Frank said. He remembered Tamara saying she lived on a lake.

"Yeah," Sara said. "She said she was really good at it. And it was this fun thing she used to do with her sisters. So I had this idea to find some water skis so that when we went out on the boat today, she'd be able to show off a little. I knew the other girls would think she was really cool."

Joe scratched his head. Sara's story was starting to make sense, except for one thing. "Why did you take *my* skis? And what happened to the other one?"

"I didn't realize they were yours until after you came to our cabin," Sara said. "Tamara told me you were asking about them, and that's when I realized.

I didn't know, I promise I didn't. They were in the shed with all the life vests. I just thought they were part of the supplies for the different cabins."

Frank nodded. "Why did you take the skis late at night, though?"

Sara put her chin in her hands. "I just wanted it to be a surprise. I snuck out after Tamara went to sleep. I brought the skis down to the boat . . . and that's when it happened."

She bit her lip, like she was afraid to go on.

"What is it?" Joe asked. "What's wrong?"

Sara's eyes filled with tears. "I'm really sorry," she said. "I brought the skis down to the boat, but when I went to put them inside it, one fell. Before I could jump in and get it, it started floating out into the lake. It was so dark . . . I lost it."

Joe let out a deep breath. It was even worse news than when he had found out the skis were gone. This meant one was gone forever. It wasn't stolen, or lost . . . it was somewhere out on the lake. He'd never see it again. What good were water skis if you only had one?

Sara started to cry now. "I'm really sorry," she said, looking at Joe. "I really am."

Joe knew that she was. She looked more upset than ever. He tried to remind himself that she'd only been trying to help her friend. She'd wanted to cheer up Tamara. "It's okay," he said. "I know you were trying to do something good."

Sara stared at her feet. "I hid the other ski because I was hoping . . . ," she said. "I don't know. I was hoping someone would find it or something."

"At least we know what happened now," Frank said.

Chet was staring at the lake. The boat with the light was getting closer. He waved to his dad, who was steering it. "You're back!" he called.

Mr. Morton pulled into the dock. A few kids got out. Some of them were red from being in the sun all morning. Others had towels slung around their necks. "We missed you guys!" Ellie said as she stepped out of the boat. "It wasn't the same without you."

"We have some good news and some bad news," Mr. Morton said. "Which one do you want first?"

Joe glanced sideways at his brother. "The good news?" he said, feeling suddenly nervous.

"We found something of yours," Mr. Morton said, and smiled. He held up the missing water ski.

"My ski!" Joe cried. He took it from Mr. Morton's hand. "This is amazing!"

Mr. Morton continued, "But you haven't heard the bad news yet. We only found one. It was floating out on the lake . . . all alone."

"He only needs one!" Frank laughed. He patted his brother on the back. Joe was practically jumping up and down, he was so excited.

"What do you mean?" Mr. Morton asked. The rest of the group looked confused.

Chet laughed. "It's a long story," he said. "We can tell it to you at lunch."

The boys started up the shore, Sara following close behind them. Joe kept looking at the water ski in his hand. He couldn't believe he'd really gotten it back.

"It's your lucky day," Frank whispered to him.

Joe was smiling so much, his face hurt. "It really is," he said.

"WOOO-HOOOO!" Joe cried. "THIS IS AMAZING!!"

The wind whipped through his hair. He zipped over the water, holding on tight to the handle. All the kids in the boat cheered.

It was Sunday morning, and they had one whole day to be on the water. The boat was packed. Frank, Chet, Sara, and Tamara had all come along for the ride. Joe had let Tamara go first. She turned out to be a great water-skier. She didn't fall once.

Suddenly Joe found himself losing speed and let go of the handles. As the boat slowed down to come back and pick him up, he floated in the water. His life vest came up around his chin, and he bobbed in the cool lake. When the boat circled back to Joe, he grinned.

"This has been one of the best days ever," he declared.

Frank reached down, helping his brother up the metal ladder. Joe grabbed a towel from the bench and sat beside him. "You bet it is. We found your skis, the sun is shining, and we have the whole rest of the day to hang out here before we have to go back home."

"Lake Poketoe is even better than I imagined," Joe said.

The boat picked up speed again. Mr. Morton turned the wheel left, directly into a small wave. All the kids cheered as they bumped up and down in their seats. Frank and Joe cheered the loudest, happy to finally be catching some sunshine.

Chet came over and handed them some iced tea, then got some for himself. He held his glass in the air in a toast. "Good job, guys," he said with a smile. He clinked it against theirs. "Another case solved!"

Don't miss the next

HARDY BOYS
Clue Book:

#4 TALENT SHOW TRICKS

Nine-year-old Frank Hardy sat in the school auditorium, going over a big checklist in a binder.

"Hey, Frank!" Chet Morton, Frank's best friend, waved from the stage. "Check this out!" Chet held up three microphones and pretended to juggle them. "Maybe I can be in the talent show too!"

Frank laughed. He'd been chosen as a Bayport Backstage Buddy member for the school's yearly talent show. That meant he was going to help with anything people needed during the show and make sure everything ran smoothly. He even had his own walkie-talkie to help in talking with everyone around the auditorium. Mrs. Castle, the music and arts teacher who directed the show, said she picked Frank to work with her because he was so organized and reliable. He didn't want to let her or the students in the show down!

The kids in the show, including his eight-year-old brother, Joe, were in the restrooms, changing into their costumes. Rehearsal would start in just a few minutes. It was Monday, and the show was at the end of the week, so they had a lot of work to do!

Frank took a few moments to check in with the rest of the BBB crew. First he talked with Eli Ramsay through the walkie-talkie, who was helping to work the lights up in a booth above the stage, and made sure he was ready to go. Then he checked on Chet, who was at the back of the auditorium. Chet was going to help with the sound—making sure each act had the right music and making sure the micro-phones all worked.

"Hey, Chet," Frank called out. His friend was

half hidden behind a huge panel with all sorts of buttons and levers. "You ready to go?"

"You bet!" Chet said, flashing Frank a thumbs-up. "You know, this stuff is pretty cool. Maybe I'll be a sound designer someday. Or a DJ!"

Frank grinned. Chet was always picking up new hobbies. As he walked away from the sound booth, he grabbed the walkie-talkie that was clipped to his jeans.

"Come in, Speedy," he said.

The walkie-talkie crackled, and the voice of his friend Cissy "Speedy" Zermeño squawked over the line. "I'm hearing you loud and clear, Frank!"

"How are things looking back there?" he asked. Speedy was also helping backstage, making sure everyone was ready to go before their act.

"We're ready to go when you are!" Speedy said.

Now that he'd checked in with the crew, Frank looked around the auditorium to see if the student director had arrived yet. Olivia Shapiro was an eighth-grade drama student from Bayport Middle School, which was just down the street. At that moment,

Olivia and her seventh-grade assistant, Zoe, came sweeping into the auditorium. Olivia's face was red and both girls were out of breath. It looked like they both ran from the middle school. Plus, although it was a warm day outside, Olivia always insisted on wearing a scarf wrapped dramatically around her neck. Frank had heard her tell Zoe in a rehearsal last week that all the great directors wore scarves.

Olivia took her usual seat in the auditorium with Zoe beside her. Zoe handed her a bottle of water, a notebook, and a pen while Olivia fanned herself.

Frank went up to Olivia. "Everyone's ready to start."

"Thank you, Frank," she said. "Can you call the cast to the stage, please? I want to talk with them before we begin."

"Sure," Frank said. He got Speedy on the walkie-talkie and told her to send the cast out. Slowly, students started to trickle onto the stage. Most were dressed in colorful costumes or fancy clothes. Some held props, like Joe, who was clutching the half-dozen orange balls he juggled in his act. Others carried instruments, like the new kid at Bayport, Ezra Moore, who held his violin and bow.

"Attention, everyone!" Olivia said, waving her hand to get the cast's attention. "I have an announcement to make."

The students stopped their chattering and turned toward their student director.

"I want to remind all of you to have your friends and family book their tickets for Friday's show now," Olivia said. "You don't want them to end up without a seat, do you?"

The cast shook their heads.

"Please feel free to see me after today's rehearsal for more tickets if you need them," Mrs. Castle chimed in. She was watching from the back of the auditorium.

"Okay, then. You'll remind them tonight when you get home." Olivia clapped her hands. "Places, please!" Frank saw a few kids roll their eyes. Olivia could be pretty bossy, and not everyone liked that!

The students scattered into the wings at the sides of the stage. The first and last numbers of the evening were songs that Olivia had choreographed herself, and they featured everyone in the show. Frank took his usual place in a seat behind Olivia and Zoe and got out his walkie-talkie.

"Eli," he said. "Can you bring up the lights for the opening number?"

"Roger, boss!" Eli radioed back. The lights in the auditorium dimmed, while those on the stage brightened.

"Chet," Frank asked, "is the music for the opening number ready to go?"

"Whenever you are, Frank," Chet replied.

"Speedy," Frank said, "is everyone in position backstage?"

"We're ready!" she said.

Frank leaned forward to tell Olivia they were ready to start, but she was deep in conversation with Zoe.

". . . think it's going to be okay," Zoe was saying to Olivia. "I heard Mrs. Castle say that over half the tickets have already been sold."

"Okay isn't good enough," Olivia said. "I want

to be a professional director someday, and this is my first chance to prove myself. This show has to sell out. What happens if they take the show away from me? Then what will I do next year?"

"Um, Olivia?" Frank interrupted. "Everyone's ready to start when you are."

"I'm ready," Olivia said. "Let's go."

"Chet," Frank said into his walkie-talkie, "start the music. Eli, hit the lights. Here we go, everybody!"

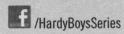